Ginny's parents were farmers on the land inherited from her grandfather.

Ginny's grandfather and great-grandfather cleared the farming areas years ago. Corn was their main crop.

Now, Ginny's parents plant corn and soybeans. They have a vegetable garden, and Ginny helps to pull the weeds.

Ginny was five years old when she became ill. None of her family's home remedies made her feel better. Ginny felt worse each day. One morning, Ginny's mom told her they were going to town to carry her to a real doctor.

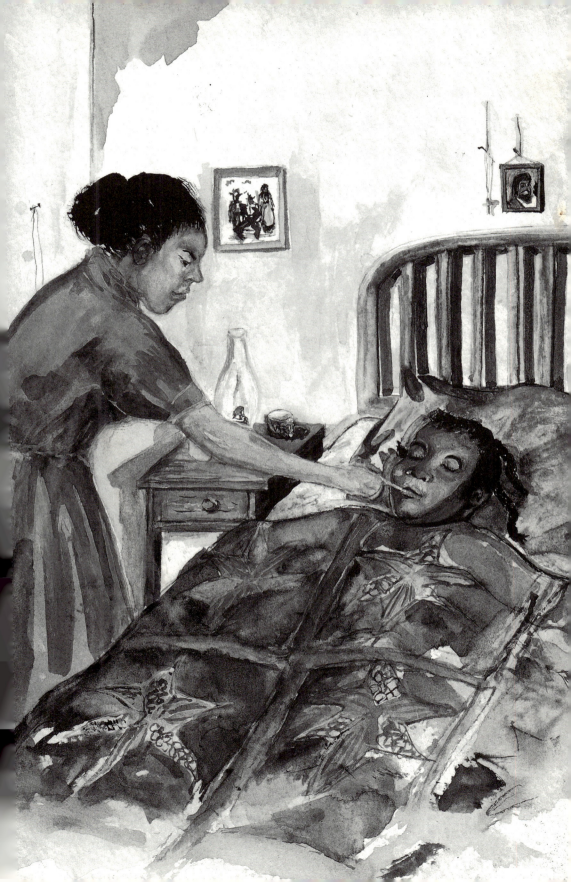

Ginny was too sick to be excited. She slept most of the way, even over rough, deeply-rutted, wet, muddy swampland roads.

The ride lasted several hours as the mule pulled the wagon through the countryside.

Ginny was glad when they reached the doctor's office. Her father carried her inside.

The doctor asked many questions as he examined Ginny. He decided that she should be taken to the hospital in his car.

Ginny had never seen a hospital room or a nurse. She noticed the smiling faces of everyone who entered her room.

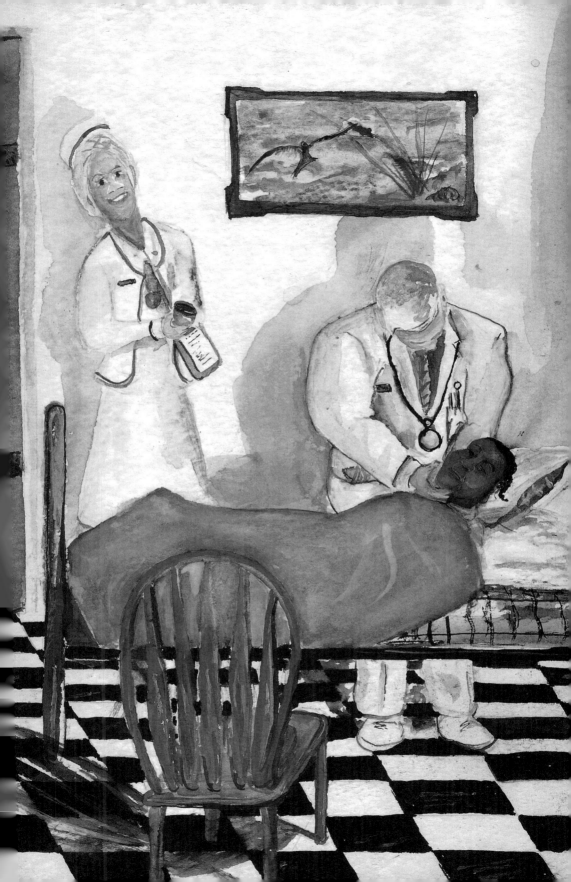

They were nice, however, Ginny longed to see her mom and dad.

She wanted to know how long it would take for her illness to go away.

A few days later, Ginny was allowed to sit in a chair by the window. It was a cloudy morning. While she sat there, a light drizzle of rain began.

As people passed by, Ginny noticed a lady walking in the rain while holding a strange object over her head.

Ginny had NEVER seen anything like that!

She was so excited that she called the nurse to share what she had seen. The nurse explained to Ginny that what she saw was an <u>umbrella</u>.

Ginny was fascinated! She absolutely had to hold an umbrella in her hands. She wanted to touch one for herself.

Ginny could not wait for her parents to come the next day!

Ginny did not want to talk to her parents about being sick; she wanted to talk about umbrellas.

She wanted an umbrella of her own.

When Ginny's nurse learned that her parents were not able to buy an umbrella, she talked to the other nurses.

They all agreed to give money toward buying Ginny her very own umbrella.

They gave so much that two colorful umbrellas were bought to brighten Ginny's eyes and her room!

Ginny sat in the chair holding her new red umbrella over her head. Then, she sat in the chair holding the new yellow umbrella over her head.

All Ginny seemed to do was smile!

As the damp misty rain continued, she noticed more and more people carrying umbrellas.

Ginny was so happy. She wanted to share the joy. She decided that she would bring joy to others with <u>Happy Umbrellas</u>. How could she do this?

For several days Ginny thought of nothing else.

Ginny had become so fascinated with umbrellas that she forgot that she was ill.

As Ginny was busy planning to bring joy to others, her own health improved each day.

Ladies of the Hospital's Auxiliary became aware of Ginny's project. They began collecting old, faded umbrellas.

The box in the corner of Ginny's room was soon overflowing.

Also, there were colorful scraps of cloth, buttons, needles and thread, glue, scissors, lace, ribbon, beads, and more!

GINNY'S UMBRELLAS

402

GINNY'S
UMBRELLAS

Ginny took the ugliest and most faded umbrella from the box and began cutting and gluing.

That old umbrella was alive with color in a matter of minutes!

Ginny asked her nurse if there were other children her age or younger in the hospital. There were!

A little girl just a few days short of five years old was in a room down the hall from Ginny.

    Ginny asked permission to give the little girl the first umbrella that she completed.

The nurse took Ginny, in a wheelchair, to deliver the umbrella to the young patient.

The little girl's name was Clara. She was overjoyed to receive such a lovely gift, especially from another little girl!

Ginny was able to leave the hospital the next day. She had recovered from her illness and was feeling much better!

    Now, Ginny was going home. She had wonderful stories to tell! She had strange and beautiful things to show!

Ginny's joy from decorating the umbrellas could not match the lovely smiles of those who received them!

As time passed, Ginny continued to spread joy by giving away <u>Happy Umbrellas.</u>